This book is for

_____,

no matter what.

For Michael and Jameson,
who never drooled, burped, or stank,
and who definitely did NOT inspire this book—LHH

To Pax, Adelynn, and Ava—
my favorites night and day, 24-7—SH

# WARTS AND ALL

*A Book of Unconditional Love*

Lori Haskins Houran

pictures by
Sydney Hanson

Albert Whitman & Company
Chicago, Illinois

So here's the thing.
I love you.

And not just when
you're sweet and cuddly

or fresh from the bath

or dressed up
in your Sunday best.

I love you *all the time.*
Day and night.

I'm talking 24-7, 365.

Even first thing in the morning,
when you can be...
oh, I don't know,
just a *touch* prickly.

I love you when you're shy

or grouchy

or wound up

or worn down.

And it doesn't matter what you do, either.

You can sneeze.

You can drool.

You can burp.

You can...
Oh.
Hoo, boy.

I can't lie—some things
are a bit tough to take.

But it's OK! Really!

Because I adore you anyway.
In every way.

Don't look so surprised!
It's true!

What I'm getting at here
is that I love you, honey.

I love you, warts and all.

And I always will.